The King's Messenger

By Campbell Eden

Illustrated by Hayden Emelia

D1521706

This book is dedicated to my fellow dyslexics who helped make The King's Messenger possible. You gathered around and helped create the book everyone with this learning disability deserves. From one dyslexic to many others, thank you for helping The King's Messenger with her story.
-Campbell Eden

CHAPTER 1

This is a story about danger, secrets, and magic. This story is also about fairies, but not the kind you might think.

These fairies have powerful minds and brave hearts. They live out stories that are almost too good to be true. Their wings glow with magic, like the moon. But it's their powers that set them apart.

Where do they live, you might ask?

Well, the fairies in this story were from a kingdom far away. They lived on an island with mermaids, trolls, and all kinds of lost things. It was far off, but still home to some brave humans, too. It was all beautiful, but nothing on the island compared to the fairies' hidden home.

The Hills of Holly was a magical place to live. A castle was hidden in the branches of a tree that grew on the edge of the island. The ocean splashed behind the castle, and the water was filled with fish and old wood from lost ships. If you were lucky, jewels could be found in the waves, too.

Other fairies lived on this island, but no kingdom was more powerful than the Hills of Holly. King Flint was known for his humor and strong will. More than anything, he wanted to see his fairies safe and happy. All his life, he watched closely over his kingdom. But this story is not about the great king.

No, this is an adventure about magic and the king's messenger.

So if you are ready, I'll begin....

Twig was leaning back in her chair. Her green eyes were shut tight, and her red curls formed a messy bun on her head. Her snores filled the warm air of the small room. Her office was at the bottom of the Hills of Holly.

Her desk was made of a flat pinecone and a smooth piece of bark. On top of it, a small sign was carved with the words: Messenger of the Hills.

Twig was smaller than most fairies. But her love of her job, and the danger that came with it, made up for her size.

Being a messenger was a dangerous and very important job. A messenger passed through great forests, human villages, pirate caves, and more. Twig was known to be the best messenger in all the land. There were other fairy kingdoms in Bridgewood and on islands nearby. A messenger was called whenever a gift or letter needed to be sent.

Twig's snores were still filling the air when a fairy burst through the door.

"Hey, Twig!" Gus shouted as he shut the door behind him. He was covered in black dust from the mine where he worked.

Twig slowly opened one glaring eye. Her cheek was still bruised from her last trip to Mermaid Cove. She was supposed to be catching up on sleep now. "What, Gus?"

"I found this and thought I should give it to you." Gus gasped for breath and dropped a small pack on her desk. It was made of silky leaves but covered in dirt.

She opened her other eye. "What is it?"

Gus shrugged. "I don't know, but it has a kingdom seal on it. I found it by the mines, which aren't near anything. I've got no idea where it came from."

Twig pulled her feet off the desk and wiped a layer of dirt off the bag. She stared at the dirty kingdom seal. This bag was meant to be in King Flint's palace, or it was sent from the kingdom and never reached its new home. Twig sniffed it. "What's in it?"

"No idea. And frankly, I don't want to know. There is too much magic in these lands for my taste."

"Says the fairy using his wings to cover my floor in dust," Twig pointed out.

Gus only laughed and pulled the door open. "I trust you with that, Twig. But I've got to get back to the mine." He shivered as he gave the bag one more look.

"Then go." Twig didn't bother looking up as he disappeared. She was too caught up in this new mystery.

Clearly, the bag had been lost or buried, but was that on purpose or by mistake?

As a messenger, Twig never asked what she was delivering. She could always trust it to be a letter, a rare gift, or much needed medicine. However, this delivery made Twig very curious. With the tip of her blade, Twig flicked the top of the bag open. A glow reflected in her eyes as she looked down. It was a plant. One small enough she could hold, with vines and dark purple flowers.

"What..." Twig had never seen a plant like this. The glow of the petals was a sign that it was still alive, despite being pulled from the dirt. This was no ordinary flower. Twig turned and grabbed an old book off her dusty shelf. She flipped through the pages but found nothing like the flower. After tearing through every book on her shelf, Twig was sure it was magic. It was not the soft, innocent kind of power that brought the sun up in the sky. This was the magic of something alive, a living thing that belonged to her king.

Twig shut the bag and grabbed her sword. It looked like sleep would have to wait. Judging by the smile on her lips as she flew out the door, Twig didn't mind one bit.

CHAPTER 2

King Flint's castle sat high above the fairy homes and buildings in the trunk of the biggest tree in the kingdom. It was a beautiful sight. The tree was big enough that a human man could fit inside its walls.

Windows made of sea glass let the fairy guards watch the busy kingdom below. The big doors of the castle were strong enough to hold off a grizzly bear.

Twig met a guard at the palace entrance. She was thankful this guard wasn't one of her brothers or her father. Twig never talked about it, but she came from a long line of brothers who were guards for the king.

Every boy in her family had picked their own path. They had all believed Twig would end up teaching flying lessons or raising fireflies. Both were good choices, but not ones that Twig wanted for herself. Her whole family had tried to make the choice for her. Her father, who was also a guard, had never thought Twig could be a messenger for the king. He certainly never thought she would outshine him. But outshine, she did.

She showed the guard her badge and the bag in her arms. He wrote something down on the leaf scroll in his hands. "And your gift?" He nodded to Twig's wrist, where she wore her bracelet.

This guard was new. Otherwise, he would have recognized Twig and already known her gift. She usually met a fairy named Nap at this door, but more and more guards had been moved around over the last few weeks. Twig guessed they were training away from the kingdom like her father and brothers sometimes did.

Twig held up her wrist. One bracelet was different from the rest. It was metal and cold. It had a drawing of the kingdom on one side and a fairy's face on the other. Every fairy in The Hills of Holly wore a bracelet like this. The face showed one of the six emotions that the fairies had the gift of control over.

All fairies were born with three special features: pointed ears, wings, and a special gift. Disgust, fear, anger, surprise, happiness, and sadness were all strong emotions. Every fairy could control one. Twig had the power of disgust. There was no rule about using your gift on yourself. But all fairies shared the fear of losing themselves in the magic like some had. The greatest crime was for a fairy to use their gift on another fairy without them knowing.

She held her bracelet up for the guard to see. The bracelets let the fairies know who had each gift. This kept them from getting tricked.

Because a fairy shouldn't use their magic on another without asking, and it was dangerous to use it on yourself, Twig never paid much attention to such things. Not many had the gift of disgust. Surprise and anger were the most common. Even without magic, Twig had never had trouble getting other fairies to stay out of her way.

The guard nodded and handed Twig the leaf he'd been writing on. The king never met someone without a leaf scroll. On it, her gift was listed. She flew quickly past the guard and through the castle. She passed sea glass windows and rugs made of unicorn hair.

Finally, she stopped before the great throne room. Twig had been here often, but the room had never been so empty before. Only the king and two of his helpers sat at the end of the long room. Normally, at least ten fairies stood beside the king. Twig stopped before the king's throne and bowed.

"Rise, child." King Flint's warm and welcoming voice echoed off the walls. Like always, he sounded excited to see her. In all her time as a messenger, the king had never grown tired of welcoming fairies into his home. Her wings flapped as she rose.

"Sir, I have a bag." Twig held up the bag and opened the top, showing the king the glowing plant. "A miner found this and brought it to my office."

King Flint suddenly looked white. He cleared his throat and leaned forward on his throne. "Ah, well, that's a very interesting plant you have." He cleared his throat again.

Twig blinked at the king's odd behavior. Still, she went on. "Yes, it is. The bag has a kingdom seal, and none of the plants in my books look like this one."

"Odd, very odd," the king swallowed. "And you are sure it doesn't match anything in your books?"

"Yes, my king...this plant has magic inside of it." Twig waited for surprise or excitement, but that's not how the king looked.

Instead, he nodded quickly as if this happened all the time. "Yes, well, thank you very much for bringing this to the castle, Twig."

She looked from the king to the two fairies beside him. They looked scared. All eyes were locked on the plant in her hands. Twig went on. "Sir...this clearly didn't come from the castle. Which means it was sent here from another place. Its magic could be dangerous. I can take it to the guards if you need-"

"No, no!" The king quickly jumped up. He rubbed his shaking hands together. "I-I do recognize the plant now. It's a thank you gift for the kingdom of Blue Hollow. I thought it would get to the Hollow last month. One of the other messengers must have dropped it."

Twig looked down at the bag in her hands. "It's for the Blue Hollow?" She had made the trip to the Blue Hollow kingdom plenty of times, and so had all the other messengers. She didn't think any of them would have dropped a bag like this.

The king forced a laugh. "Yes, its magic may seem powerful, but it is only as strong as the dust on your wings."

Twig nodded, but she couldn't help thinking that the magic in this bag felt much stronger than her own. "I've traveled the path to the Blue Hollow dozens of times, my king. I can have it there in a few days. I'm sure the fairies there have been waiting for it."

The fairies in Blue Hollow were very strict about thank you gifts arriving on time. Twig didn't like the idea of a messenger dropping a delivery. She would feel restless until everything was made right.

"No, no!" the king shouted. "I mean, no child. You just returned from another trip."

Twig nodded slowly. Again, she looked at the other fairies for an answer to the king's odd behavior. They only kept their eyes on the plant. "Yes sir, but I am more than willing to set this right-"

"Please, rest, child. Leave the bag with Fredrick here, and I will send another messenger," the king said.

Twig frowned. She didn't want another messenger taking this job. Not if the bag had already been lost once. She trusted her own skills more than anyone else. "Truly, sir, I insist that I take care of this mission. Let me fix-"

The king cut her off. "Okay...my child. Of course, you can fix this." He forced a smile. "But please, rest a few days and then come back here. You will be the one to bring the plant to the Blue Hollow."

Something was wrong with the king, or this bag. Twig saw it in his eyes and on the faces of the other fairies. She hid her confusion behind a quick nod. "Yes, Your Majesty. I'll be back in a few days."

"Please, take your time, a week if you need." King Flint seemed relieved that she had agreed to rest. He waved a hand to the fairy at his side. "Fredrick here will hold on to the bag for you." One of the fairies rushed forward and smiled as he took the bag. He seemed just as relieved as the king.

Twig looked from one to the other. Something about all of this was wrong. Twig saw clearly that the king was lying to her. She never remembered him doing such a thing.

With nothing left to say, Twig nodded and turned to fly out of the room. Hushed whispers from the fairies echoed off the walls as she pushed through a doorway.

"Get that bag to Bo right away." The door shut just as the king's words met her pointed ears.

Twig froze. Bo was not a guard or a messenger. He was the king's son.

CHAPTER 3

Twig shivered as she flew out of the castle. Everything about her meeting with the king was wrong. Her head spun as she fluttered past shops and fairies on her way back to her office.

She slammed the door behind her and looked down at the books on her desk. She bit her lip. Why did the king want the bag given to his son? She pictured Bo. He and Twig had only met a handful of times.

Bo was about her age. He was incredibly quiet and respectful. Bo was gifted with one of the most common emotions: surprise. His head was covered in brown curly hair like his father, with brown eyes to match. His skin was tan. His big body always reminded her of a rock. Twig was a smaller fairy, but Bo was twice her size.

He was not a guard or a messenger. Bo was the future king. She ran her fingers over the pages of the old books. The king had said she could take care of the plant. But only after she had agreed to rest for a few days. She bit her lip again, thinking the king was lying about something.

Twig began stacking the books. He was lying. He was scared. And he had ordered the bag to be given to Bo. A guard should have held the bag until Twig was ready to deliver it. So, the plant wasn't where it should have been.

Twig's hands froze. It was starting to look like she wouldn't be the one taking the plant to the Blue Hollow. Twig was the best messenger in the whole kingdom. It went against everything in her to let another fairy deliver the bag.

King Flint had told her she would be the one to take care of the bag, but he had given it to his son. The Blue Hollow had already been waiting for the plant for a month. "The king is going to have it delivered without me." The hushed words left Twig's lips, and she was sure of them. "He lied about letting me deliver the bag."

Why? She had no idea. The only thing Twig knew was that she hated anyone else stealing her job, her duty to the kingdom.

She didn't need rest. If this was about the king's trust, she had every right to prove to him that he should trust her. If the bag was being delivered without her, she knew it could leave the castle at any time.

Twig looked out the little window of her fairy sized office. The sun had almost set. If the bag were leaving the kingdom tonight, she wouldn't have time to find the messenger before they left.

Twig threw a hand drawn map across her desk. She stabbed the biggest path with her knife. She knew the trail to the Blue Hollow by heart. It started right outside of the kingdom. The road went on for some time before cutting off into different paths. Some paths went deeper into the woods, some crossed caves and beaches, and some never ended.

She would watch the trail tonight. If no one passed by with the bag, she would look for the other messengers first thing in the morning.

A lot of fairies knew Twig by her fiery spirit. She was protective of the job she had earned. While she didn't always look like the sweetest fairy, she had a golden heart. Twig would never hurt another fairy. But she would not back down if one got in the way of her duty. Twig was not a fairy that broke easily.

She flew around the room, pulling on her suit of armor. It was made of nut shells that her mother had tied together. She also wrapped pieces of leather around her small feet. She filled her pockets with tools and food.

In a flash, she was ready and flying past little fairy homes. They were carved out of wood or built in the branches of trees. Fireflies lit up the small houses. Tiny clouds of smoke filled the air as she passed the baker's shop.

Some fairies might choose to have small lives, but if they put their minds to it, there were very few things their magic couldn't do.

Twig flew for some time through the village before the shops and mills were behind her. She found the trail and hid behind a bush. She could see anyone who came past. Twig tucked her wings against her little body and pulled a leaf across her shoulders, hiding the glow of her magic.

With the sun gone, the moon was slowly rising higher and higher. She waited as hour after hour passed. Still, Twig trusted herself. She knew she was right about the king's plan.

She sucked on a piece of dried fruit and jumped as a unicorn crossed her path. The animal was white as snow, and its horn glowed with a pink light as it walked past the bush. It disappeared just as soon as it came.

She was starting to wonder if the bag really was leaving the castle tonight. But then, a soft light appeared up the trail. Twig watched as a single fairy walked down the path. She held her leaf tightly against her body. The fairy was coming toward her with a bag on their back.

CHAPTER 4

Twig waited until the fairy passed by her bush. Then she asked, "Who is there?"

The fairy froze as Twig stepped out from behind the bush and onto the path. He was a head taller than Twig, and his body reminded her of a rock.

He was wearing the bag on his back. His wings cast a glow on the path. "I'm a royal guard from the kingdom of the Hills of Holly. You are blocking my way," he said.

Twig had never seen this guard before. The hood covering his head made it impossible to see his eyes. He looked past her, searching the dark path.

She watched him closely. "Well, I'm the king's messenger, and it's never a guard's job to deliver a bag like that." She stepped closer. The knife she had tied to her hip was now in her small hand. "So I'll ask you again, who are you?"

"A guard of the king," he said again, but he didn't sound sure himself.

Twig looked at the bag. This was her job, it was her duty. The king had let someone else do her job and Twig wasn't even sure he was a real guard. "Like I said, guards do not make deliveries like this. This is a messenger's job." She pointed her knife at the bag. "My job."

The big fairy looked down at Twig, then again at the dark woods. He was nervous.

"Hey, I'm talking to you." She tapped the edge of his hood with her knife. A fairy her size should have been afraid as he looked down on her, but not Twig.

Something about all of this was not right. Twig hated being in the dark. Right now, she hated that the dark was exactly where she found herself. Her king didn't trust her to make the delivery or with the job she had earned in the kingdom.

The big fairy hissed down at her. "Shhhh." Then he looked around the dark woods again. "I'm working for the king. You should go back home, messenger." He cleared his throat. He sounded sorry, but he didn't say he was.

Twig pulled her shoulders back. Her glare would have scared anyone else, but not this fairy. He simply looked sorry. And...scared.

He wasn't scared of Twig but of the woods around them. She wrinkled her nose and glared at him. "Why are you taking that plant in the dead of night?" She pointed her knife at the bag.

He froze. He didn't know what to do with the fairy glaring up at him. He needed to keep moving to get this plant away from the kingdom. He shoved her knife out of the way and lied to her. "I don't know what you're talking about. Now, please, go home, messenger." He really was sorry, but more than that, he didn't want Twig out in these woods. It was not safe, not now.

He went around her and started to fly. But Twig wasn't done with him yet. She flew up and quickly used her knife to cut the bag off his back. He spun in the air. Fairy dust fell from their wings as she flew past him. High above the trail, they faced each other.

Twig hugged the bag to her body. She had too many questions to let this fairy leave with the plant. "I'll ask again: What are you doing with this?" She held up the bag.

He spun wildly and looked around the woods. "I-I told you, I work for the king. Now give me the bag." He was nervous and lying. He sounded just like the king.

"You are lying," she said.

"You need to be quiet," he hissed.

"No." Twig insisted. "I don't know who you are. But I know that this is too powerful for you to have." She tied the bag to her waist and held out her knife.

He groaned and rubbed a hand down his covered face. "Fine." He ripped the hood off, and Twig gasped at the sight of Bo.

"You are the king's son," she said. Before she had time to think, a branch snapped. Twig spun around. Bo grabbed her just as another set of wings flew past her ear.

CHAPTER 5

Bo and Twig rolled through the air. They crashed into the dirt and landed in a pile of dust. The magic in their wings and the moon above them was the only light on the dark path.

Twig pushed Bo off of her. They lay beside each other, gasping for air. Suddenly, another fairy landed on Twig's chest.

Everything happened so quickly.

Four fairies attacked Twig and Bo. They were dressed in raven feathers, and their wings were covered in leaves. Twig gasped as one hit her jaw. She hit back and rolled the moaning fairy off of her chest.

Bo threw another off the trail. Twig stumbled to her feet, ready for another attack. Blood dripped off her lips. The bag hung from her waist. Bo stumbled back, falling into Twig. They righted themselves as hissing filled the air.

The four fairies were circling them.

"Who are you?" Twig asked the dark fairies as she spun around. She pulled her knife out. She had never been attacked by a group like this.

The dark fairies were circling. Bo was standing as close to Twig as he could. "Protect the plant at all costs," he hissed. Bo charged. His wings glowed as he threw one of the dark fairies into a bush.

Twig felt someone before she could see them. Bo was fighting off two more dark fairies while she spun around. Twig met the last dark fairy. They both stood frozen.

She held her knife to his neck. "Step off." Twig bit out. She was holding the bag with one hand and the knife with the other. Blood was still running down her lip. She could hear the other fairies fighting behind her. Groans came from the bush.

"You first," the dark fairy said as he laughed. His eyes were black. His hair was dark, and...suddenly, Twig had never felt more scared.

It felt like another fairy had gone inside of her and turned off her joy. Her heart hurt, and tears rolled down her face. They mixed with the blood, and she fell to the ground. She cried out for help, for anything to make the fear stop.

Something grabbed her neck. She stabbed blindly with her knife. She was screaming, begging.

Then...it all stopped, like water on a fire.

Someone groaned. Twig spun on her knees. Her wings filled the darkness with their glow. Her knife was raised high and dripped with blood. Twig gasped for air as she looked around the trail. Her wings cast a glow on the bloody dirt.

Bo was rising to his feet slowly. His hands held out to her. His eyes said something Twig could not read.

One dark fairy still groaned in the bush. Two more laid on the ground. She spun, looking for the one who had attacked her—the one who had laughed at her knife.

The ground was bare. The last dark fairy was gone. Only a pool of blood sat where he had been.

Bo spoke. "He disappeared. Down the trail, back towards the kingdom."

Twig jumped at his words. Now, coldness had filled her. She nodded slowly and lowered her knife.

Bo pointed to the plant. "You protected the plant. Thank you." She nodded again and looked down at the bag still tied to her. The flower still glowed; it was perfectly safe. His voice was low, but sure. "You can not go back now."

Her head spun around. "What?"

"I...we can't go back now." Bo swallowed his fear and kicked at the dirt. Moans from the other fairies filled the air.

Twig dabbed at the blood on her lip with a shaking hand and met his dark eyes. "We need to go after him. He attacked the son of the king." She stumbled to her feet.

"No!" He shook his head and reached for her arm. He pulled her past the fairies on the ground and started to run.

"No!" Twig ripped her hand from his. She forced him to face her. She didn't feel as sure as she sounded. Her fear from before was still making her hands shake. "What are you doing with this plant?" Twig wondered if Bo could be trusted.

"I-I." Bo seemed unsure of himself. He knew a little about Twig, but only from what he had heard about her. Twig took her job as a messenger very seriously. Because of that, now she was bleeding and stuck with him. "I can not explain everything now, but I can say I'm on a mission for my father. I am pressed for time. I am delivering this plant-"

"You are delivering this to the Blue Hollow." Twig glared up at him. Why should the king's son be trusted with her job?

He shook his head. "No. Not the Blue Hollow."

Twig froze. "Then where? And why you? All alone like this?" A fairy on the ground groaned and started to open its eyes.

"We need to leave." Bo grabbed her arm.

She stumbled along with him down the path. "Where are you going? And why can't we go back? Why can't we go after...him?" She pointed to the pool of blood behind them.

He looked over at her as the moans of the dark fairies faded from earshot. "This plant is magic. You were right. It's far stronger than my father wanted anyone to know. It is needed somewhere else." Bo's big chest puffed out as he looked around the dark path.

Before he left the castle, his father had wished him luck and warned him about the woods. Now, every snap of a branch sounded like another pack of danger.

Twig shivered as her own screams echoed in her ears. "Why can't we go after...that fairy? If he's going to the kingdom, we need to warn them. He's...powerful."

Bo turned to her. His big shoulders blocked her from the cold wind. "My father knows there is a chance of an attack. Right now, I can not turn back. I have to get this plant where it is needed. I won't let you go back out there alone, not when there could be more dark fairies. Not after what he did to you."

Twig looked away. Her screams echoed in her ears.

Bo went on. "You may think you're fine, but your body will be stressed for the next few hours. You won't be able to hold off another attack like that. I will not risk sending you back and..." He looked down. Bo's father had trusted him to get this plant where it needed to go, but...he had never been the leader his father was.

He used his size and his silence to make it look like he knew more than he did. The silence also made other fairies forget about him, which was just what he wanted.

But now, Twig was standing before him. He didn't want to send her out in the dark of night, not after that fairly used his gift on her. Twig's screams were unlike anything he had ever heard. No scream had ever frozen him like hers had.

"And?" She pressed. The blood on her lips was dark under the glow of their wings.

Bo looked up and down the dark trail. "Since you are already here, I'm not too big of a fairy to say that I would like your help."

She blinked in surprise. Bo didn't know why his words made her feel that way. After seeing Twig return to the kingdom beaten and bright eyed from bringing a fresh message to his father, he always thought she was the best messenger a royal family could have.

"My help with what?" Twig asked.

Bo jumped as an owl hooted above them. "For starters, you can help me make sure I'm on the right path."

Twig lifted a brow. She really didn't like the idea of hunting down that dark fairy. And Twig was not going to pass up the offer to do her job. But... "Why did the King lie about this?" She held up the magic plant. "And why did those fairies want it so badly?"

Bo swallowed. "Because this plant is going to help stop a war, and those fairies want a battle."

Twig froze at the word war.

A branch snapped, and Bo pulled them both off the trail. He pinned her against a tree and waited. Bo watched the dark sky.

"What war?" As far as Twig knew, their kingdom had been at peace for years.

Bo was watching the sky as he answered. "Those fairies are not from the Blue Hollow or any other kingdoms you deliver to. They come from the troll lands."

"Trolls," horror filled Twig. The big creatures were known for being fairy killers.

"The dark fairies are working with the trolls. They have already taken over the Blue Hollow. There is nothing left of the kingdom you know there." Bo looked down on Twig. "That plant's magic is needed on the front lines. It's going to help stop the war."

"Front lines?"

Bo's eyes turned soft. The idea of fighting, or magic, made him sick. "Where do you think all our soldiers are?"

Twig swallowed. Suddenly, everything he was saying fell into place. The missing soldiers, the king's lies, the plant, only...Twig looked up at him. She had a firm hold on the plant as she met his dark eyes. "Why are you delivering this? The king's son of all people? You are our future king, after all."

Bo looked away. He said the first answer that came to mind. "Loyalty. The king wanted to be sure that someone he trusted was in charge of the plant." He held his breath and watched the little fairy. He waited for her to believe him.

"So the king doesn't trust me?" Hurt filled her voice, and she let him hear it.

Bo shook his head quickly. "No, no. Uh...he was worried about the part your brothers could play."

"My brothers?" she asked slowly.

He swallowed. "They...uh, he was worried that you might be thrown off by your brothers being in battle. He didn't want to put too much on you."

Their eyes met. Twig knew that Bo was lying. She stared him down. He was acting like his father had in the throne room. She believed what he had said about the war. And the dark fairies were real. But she didn't believe his reason for being out here all alone. The owl hooted again, and Bo jumped.

Twig pushed his chest away from her. "Fine. So you are the leader of this one man band. I'll help, of course, it's my duty. The question is, where are the front lines of this war?"

CHAPTER 6

For hours, Bo and Twig flew. Only their wings and the moon gave them light on the dark path. Bo didn't think asking Twig to give him the plant would do any good. Twig kept it tied to her waist as they flew through the night.

She had never been to the edge of the Hissing Woods, but she could get them most of the way. There was always fog in the Hissing Woods, making it the perfect home for trolls. The perfect place for a war. If they flew as fast as they could, the two fairies would reach the woods in a few short days.

Twig was scared to think about the trolls. She was scared of how close the fairy killers were.

As they flew above the treetops, Bo answered all of Twig's questions. Such as: "When did the war start?"

He thought for a moment and then said, "We knew a growing group of fairies were making small attacks on other kingdoms last year. Then, they all just left. We hoped it was over, but they brought an army of trolls with them to take over the Blue Hollow."

"What do the frontlines look like?" Twig asked.

"We are holding off the dark fairies and trolls. But this plant is the only thing that will stop them."

Twig looked down at the bag and lifted her eyebrow. "How magical is this?"

Bo swallowed. "It can hold off dozens of trolls."

Twig was still shaking from the dark fairy magic earlier. They were both afraid. They flew in silence until the sunrise took the place of the moon. Twig thought about the war and how the magic plant would be used.

Bo looked back every few minutes to make sure Twig was still with him. He had to force himself to stay calm every time a branch snapped. He couldn't fail this mission. He could not let his father or his people down.

Bo tried to hide his fear, but Twig could see the stress as they crossed rivers and hollow trees.

Twig watched Bo fly ahead of her. He was quiet and known for his size more than anything else. His hands were fisted, and his tanned face was covered in sweat. Bo was his father's only son and Twig's future king.

Twig remembered that his gift was the feeling of surprise, a very common bit of magic. Yet still, he was the one trusted with the plant. Shaking her head, Twig wondered why the king had not sent more fairies with Bo. Something still seemed wrong, even if Bo was the king's son.

Of course, she was right to question. She didn't know the full truth yet.

At that very moment, Bo looked back. He could feel Twig watching him. Her red curls flew in the wind as the two fairies flew around a waterfall and swooped down into a valley. Blood was still on her lip, and her face was marked on the side. Power seemed to pour out of her.

Not for the first time, Bo was glad she was with him. A mission was much lonelier than it sounded. Their eyes met. Twig wondered why Bo was hiding something from her. But Bo could only see the fear and pain in her eyes. Her screams echoed in his pointed ears. "You okay?" his deep voice asked.

She blinked her green eyes and lifted her chin. "Of course."

He nodded but did not believe her.

She went on, "We will rest in an hour by a cove."

He nodded again. There was something wrong with Twig. That much he knew. Only one reason came to mind. Bo dropped back so they could fly side by side. "Do you know what happened with the dark fairy? Back on the trail? He, uh, he used his magic on you."

Twig's eyes jumped to the bracelet on her wrist. Bo looked at it, too. Her gift was disgust.

"You said I would feel stressed for a while after?" Twig wanted to know when she would stop shaking.

He nodded. "Yes, it can take a few hours for the feelings to fade after an attack like that."

"Like that? You make it sound like one gift is different from another." Twig had never given their gifts much thought. Maybe that was a mistake.

"The more a fairy wants to use their gift on someone, the stronger it feels," Bo shrugged. He was not on edge around Twig. Shrugging was just one of his habits. It made other fairies think he was unsure of himself and helped him look more forgettable. Bo wanted to be forgettable.

Twig nodded and swallowed. "So...what gift do you think he used on me?" She kept her eyes on the trail below them.

Bo thought it was odd that a fairy wouldn't know which gift had been used on them. Then he remembered that not all fairies grew up learning how to tell the difference like he had. No one in the kingdom had grown up like him, and not because he was born in the castle. His voice was sure, "Fear. He used fear on you, and the dark fairy was serious about it."

Twig held the plant a little tighter. After hearing it from Bo, Twig would never wonder what happened on the trail that night. Twig nodded and shoved the echo of fear down. She pointed out another trail they needed to follow.

Bo acted like he didn't notice her shaking and let Twig lead. Without Twig, Bo might have missed the path. Another wave of fear hit him. They could not fail this mission. They had to get the plant to the soldiers.

"So, was it easy to tell he was using fear?" Twig asked over her shoulder. She didn't look back as she flew.

Bo's hand started to sweat. He looked around for any danger. "Yes, uh...you can tell by the screams. If it were disgust or anger, it would sound like you lost your temper. Not like you are crying for help." Bo didn't like to talk about gifts. After that, they flew in silence.

The sun was higher when Twig pointed out a willow tree where they could take a break. The plant was kept close to her side while they rested their wings.

Twig took some time to sharpen her knife. Bo ate a berry from a bush and watched her steady work. His eyes moved to the bracelet on her wrist. Disgust.

He didn't think the gift fit her very well.

She seemed much more like a fairy who would have the gift of surprise or even fear. He could see her making others afraid even without using magic. But disgust? No, he shook his head at the idea. That just didn't fit Twig.

After a while, his eyes began to slide shut. The sun was putting him to sleep.

"You can rest for a while if you'd like," Twig said without looking up.

Bo shook his head clear. "No, I'll rest when we have more cover."

Bo trusted Twig, just like he trusted his father. But that didn't mean Twig should be the only one with eyes on the plant.

"What do you call this?" She pointed to the glowing bag.

He shrugged his big shoulders. "A war stopper, a gift from above, a troll stopper...plant?"

She laughed at his words. She had never heard the king's son make a joke. Before this mission, she had never heard him say more than two words at a time.

"Just plant? It seems like it might have a type or something..." She lifted the bag to her eyes and watched the purple glow.

"I don't know if it has a type," Bo said. "I've heard plants are more of a seed and sunlight kind of thing. Not a lot of romance there."

Twig blinked up at him. When she saw the smile on his round face, she knew he was joking. She laughed again, a little surprised now. Her future king did not seem like the fairy she had guessed him to be-

"I smell a little plumb, I smell baby thumbs...."

Twig froze as Bo turned white.

She had never seen a troll, but all fairies had heard stories about troll voices.

Trolls moaned and talked with little songs.

This was the voice of a troll. "I want to beat my drum until those little fairies go numb."

Bo jumped from his branch and grabbed Twig. The two slipped and began to fall toward the ground. Twig pushed at him, but Bo only gripped harder. His wings shot out, slowing them right before they dropped to the ground.

"A troll." He hissed in Twig's ear. He held them both close to the roots of the tree.

"Why did you bring us down here?" Twig hissed back. She looked for the body that matched the booming troll voice. "And let me go-"

The branch they had been sitting on shattered as a troll crashed into the tree. Bo screamed before Twig could cover his mouth. Their wide eyes locked.

"We can't stay here," she said. Trolls were not just known for having loud voices. They had a better sense of smell than any other living thing. That meant the troll could smell them.

Bo nodded. Then his eyes got wide. He grabbed Twig's head and pulled it to his chest as wood from another broken branch fell from the sky. The troll was covered in green fuzzy skin. He wore the clothes of dead men wrapped around his neck. His bare feet stopped beside the tree.

"I smell little fairy thumbs..." The troll was old and already angry. He had just lost a unicorn in the forest. He had planned on making it his lunch. Now, his gray lips were curled as he smelled fairies in the air.

"Protect the plant-" Bo was cut off by Twig's wide eyes. He tried to spin to face the troll, but she didn't give him time. Twig pulled him back, and they rolled just as the troll's foot landed where they had been standing.

The troll laughed. "I see two little babies!"

The troll may have been big, but he was also quick. His fist landed in the dirt, creating a cloud of brown dust. Twig and Bo rolled out of the way just in time.

Twig's heart beat in her chest as the troll's fist came at them again.

"We need to fly," Bo shouted and shoved her forward.

Their wings flapped in the air-then the world seemed to spin. Twig screamed. The troll had slapped them with the tip of his big fingers. They crashed into a patch of mushrooms.

For a moment, everything was still. They were gasping as they rolled under a mushroom to hide. Twig and Bo pulled their feet to their chest.

The troll stood tall and laughed as he came towards the mushroom patch.

Twig swallowed and checked that the plant was still tied to her waist. "I've never heard of a troll being this close to the kingdom."

"Maybe he will leave us alone," Bo hoped. He sat on one knee and watched as the feet came closer. He fisted his hands and took deep breaths.

"All we need is to get away from him. Then, the troll will pick a new smell to chase. Like a unicorn or water…" Twig's voice faded as she went still. Bo froze too.

The troll was breathing deeply. Smelling. "I smell…The one who keeps the others safe…" The troll was no longer laughing. He was now hungry and even more angry.

At first, Bo and Twig did not know what his words meant.

Then Twig turned white as she held up the glowing bag. "This." One of the petals had fallen out of the bag and landed at the troll's feet. He could smell the sweetness of the flowers.

Bo fisted his hands. "For some reason, he wants the plant."

"And he won't stop following the smell," Twig finished as the truth hit them.

This plant could somehow stop a whole group of trolls. Of course, the troll would want it. Of course, he would stop at nothing to get it.

"Do you know how to use it?" Twig asked.

Bo shook his head. "No idea. But unless he is stopped here, he will not give up the hunt. Not this time."

Twig nodded and pulled her knife from her belt. She swallowed and flipped it in her small hand.

Bo spun on his knee and grabbed her arm. "Give me the plant."

She did not even look at him. "No."

"Give it to me," Bo hissed as the troll's booming steps got closer.

"No!" she snapped.

Bo moaned and thought of every way he could make her hand over the plant. He had several ideas, but only one that would work. "As your future king, I order you to give me this plant. Unless he is stopped, that troll will hunt one of us down. And it won't be you." Bo gave her his best glare.

Twig did not even look his way as she spoke. "It won't be you."

"Twig-"

She cut him off. "Unless we want to take him with us, we will have to stop the troll here."

Bo growled at her just as the top of the mushroom was ripped off. Then, he did something that would be talked about for years.

Twig was planning to run one way, and she was hoping Bo would run the other. Instead, Bo grabbed her feet, swung her around, and let her go. The extra push gave her the speed she needed to get past the troll's swinging hand.

It was a move that would be repeated many times on this island in the future. But for now, Twig was in the air. She was flying as fast as she could away from the troll.

With Bo's help, she moved quicker than ever. She made sure the troll was following her. Bo had given her a chance, and she could not waste it. Now, she needed to keep him safe, too.

Twig swooped under branches and around trees as she tried to find a way to help Bo. The troll crashed into the trees as he ran after her. Twig was slowing down...then suddenly, she saw a puddle of water.

Twig knew what to do now. She knew how to stop the booming troll behind her, how to keep the plant safe, and how to keep Bo safe.

If Twig could keep the troll following her without getting killed, she could lead him over a waterfall they had just passed. Bo and Twig could leave him there and get so far away he couldn't track them.

Twig's face always looked serious when she was sure she was doing her job. Her lips twisted, and her cheeks turned red when she was serving her king, or in this case, his son. She had that look now.

Just a little faster…just a little more, and she would have him over the edge…

The troll's big finger brushed her wing, and she gasped. A scream left her lips as she pushed herself a little faster. Just a little more…

Bo chased after the pair. He was flying as fast as he could to catch up with the troll ahead of him. He heard rushing water and felt the grin on his face as he began to see Twig's plan.

They just needed to get a little closer and…

Fear filled his gut as everything seemed to slow down. For a split second, Twig had done it. She was flying just over the cliff and would be out in the open air. The troll would fall far below into a trap of gushing water.

Only she didn't see the spider web stretched between the last two trees on the cliff. She crashed into the strings, and Bo watched as she began to fall toward the dirt.

Twig hit the ground, trapped in the strings, just short of the drop off. The troll laughed as he stood above her. She was gasping as she cut at the webs. But she could never cut the plant or herself free before the troll got them.

"No!" Bo spun around as he looked for any way to end this.

Nothing could stop the troll now. They were so close...The troll laughed and pressed his finger to Twig's head. She screamed as he played with her.

At Twig's scream, Bo swallowed and felt sick. He looked down at his hands and didn't let himself think. He had to try... He swooped down on the troll and pressed his hands to the troll's arm.

Bo slowed down and calmed his body. Then he let anger flow through his hands. The troll jumped and let out a scream of rage. He spun from Twig and beat at the air, trying to find Bo.

Bo flew at the troll again. Now, he let fear fill his hands.

The scream turned from anger to cries of help. The troll stumbled back and crashed into the two trees. He spun and ran from Bo. The troll fell right over the edge of the cliff.

A splash echoed. Bo fell to his knees and his wings gave out.

CHAPTER 7

Twig's hands shook as she cut away the last spider webs. She sat up. The plant was still safely tied to her waist. She slowly stood on shaking feet.

Bo was sitting on his knees. He was frozen and pale. Her mind could not make sense of what she had just seen. What had Bo done?

"Bo?" Her voice was unsure. When he did not say anything, she walked to him and put a hand on his arm. He was covered in sweat.

"Bo?" Her voice was harder now. Still, Bo did not answer, and his eyes were shut. She pulled on his arm and forced his chin up to meet her eyes. "Hey! Are you okay?"

"Me?" Surprise filled his voice. Then he laughed. "Me? Am I okay?"

"Yeah.." Twig looked around. She did not know why he was acting like this.

He used his wings to jump up and shook her off. "Didn't you see the troll, Twig?" He started walking back down the trail.

"You know I did." Twig glared at his back. "But we stopped it...you stopped it. I think." She followed him.

Bo folded his arms. Suddenly, his voice was low and unsure. "Yeah, I stopped him."

"How?" Twig asked as she walked with him.

"How?" He lifted his eyebrow.

She waved back towards the cliff. "Yeah, how did you do that?"

"You are very calm for what just happened," Bo said.

Twig shrugged. "It's my job to not panic in the woods."

He rolled his dark eyes. "I'm talking about how I stopped the troll."

"How *did* you stop the troll?" Twig turned so that she was walking backward and facing Bo.

"I used my gift," Bo said.

Twig shook her head. "That was not your gift."

His eyes moved to the dirt. "Yes, it was."

Bo's heart was pounding. Twig was so calm. Bo was not sure she understood what had happened. Only his father had ever seen Bo use his gifts.

Bo had all the gifts, not just one.

He had never let anyone else know that he had this much magical power. Fairies feared anyone having too much power. Being the future king, he had to be even more careful. The fairies might not trust Bo if they knew he had all the gifts. They would wonder what was stopping him from using his power on the kingdom? Bo kept his head down and waited for her eyes to darken with distrust.

Twig started to speak. "That can't be your gift, because you used more than one..." Her small voice faded as she froze.

Bo kept walking. Now Twig understood. "You have more than one gift." Her voice was low. He nodded. Twig asked slowly, "How many?"

He swallowed and didn't look back. "All six."

Her voice was clear. "That is why your father sent you alone."

He paused. "Yeah."

Now Bo waited for Twig to judge him, lash out, and change before his eyes. Twig's voice came from behind. "Smart move." Bo blinked and turned back.

She held her hands up before her chest. "Don't get me wrong, I don't like that I wasn't picked to do my job. But if my son were the future king and had your gifts, I'd keep it a secret too." She started walking towards him. "You never know when you need to save a tool to save your life."

Twig passed him, and Bo stood frozen. Twig had called Bo a tool, but that was the best he could have hoped for. A slight smile crossed his lips as he stared at her back. Just when he thought he was starting to know Twig, she threw him off again.

She called back to him, "You coming?"

"Yes." Bo sped up. "So you really are okay with me..." He shrugged, lost for words.

She was silent for a moment and then spoke. "Are you ever going to use one of those gifts on me without asking?"

Bo didn't need a second to think. "Never. Not in my lifetime. I promise."

Twig looked over at him. He had saved her life, and he had lied to her. Maybe she should be more upset or more scared. But Twig was a little proud and sometimes hard headed.

More than anything else, Twig was happy the king had a good reason for not choosing her to deliver the plant. She was at peace when she knew that her duty to the kingdom was still her own.

Bo was more powerful than any fairy she had ever known. Twig could see why Bo's father had kept him hidden from the world.

Twig nodded, "But just so you know, the next time your father thinks the fairy with six gifts is the best for the job, that doesn't mean I should not be asked to come along."

They shared a laugh. Twig's eyes sparkled with humor. "It is my job, after all. I mean, really, you should have been asking me if you could come along on this trip."

Bo laughed. His shoulders shook extra hard now that he felt free. "Now that you know about my gifts, you think you deserve to know all the royal family's secrets?"

Twig thought and then shrugged. "Why not? I am their messenger, after all."

Under her jokes, Bo could see how much she truly loved her job. "You are the messenger."

"I am. So just remind your father of that next time. Because this?" She waved a hand between them. "Is not happening again. Not unless you ask me first."

She sped up and pointed to a hidden trail they would travel until dark.

He laughed. "I'll make sure I do."

CHAPTER 8

Bo and Twig spent the next two nights watching for trolls and enjoying their newfound freedom.

Twig flew over the dark forest that was filled with sleeping unicorns. She knew she should be more unsettled by the level of power Bo had at his fingertips. But honestly, Twig was just so happy and proud to still be trusted by the king, and now his son, that she simply did not care.

On the other hand, Bo, who was flying behind Twig, was happy for the same reason. He had not felt this free in years. Long ago, when his powers were discovered, Bo and his father had known it was best to keep his gift hidden.

They had told everyone he had a common gift and tried to make it look that way. But Twig knew his secret. Bo quickly decided he did not care that she loved her job above everything else. Twig would still think of him like she always had.

He smiled because he had one more person he could trust and be himself around.

For hours, they flew together. Twig and Bo were both smiling and happy about the twist in the story. Twig admitted that she did not know where she and Bo were. She had never been this far before.

They knew that the troll's land was close. And that the Hills of Holly's army was somewhere in the fog.

Bo and Twig did not know if a great battle was happening, or if all the fairies and trolls were dead. Had the frontlines of the war moved entirely? They only knew their mission together was going to end very soon, one way or another.

"Twig." Bo's quiet voice drew her to a stop. "Look." He pointed to the dark forest below them. The fog started to wrap around their glowing wings.

"We are here." She spun in a slow circle above the forest.

"Where is the battle?" Bo asked. His hands were fisted at his waist. His wings flapped hard and quick.

Twig scanned the trees. "If there is a battle, we could not see it from here. We need to get down lower."

He nodded, and they slowly began to fly past the treetops.

Twig muttered, "I can't see anything." She had seen fog before, but never this thick.

Bo spoke, "I'm guessing you still don't have any better ideas about how to use the plant?"

She shook her head. "Nope."

They stopped and sat on a low hanging branch. Bo and Twig pressed their backs together to make their wings a little more hidden. They looked down at the dark ground below. Everything was quiet. Still.

Bo hissed as he admitted. "Twig, I don't know how to find the others. This forest is huge."

Twig was silent. She heard him, but her mind was somewhere else. She was searching the forest, the trees, and the ground.

Bo nudged her shoulder with his own. "Twig?"

"Yeah?" She answered slowly.

He nudged her again. "You okay?"

"I will be..." She lifted a finger and pointed to a hollow tree. It was deep in the wetlands of the forest. "Do you see that?"

Bo looked around but did not see anything. "No."

Twig pulled her knife from her belt. Bo knew what that meant. He fisted his hands and rose with her. She hissed in his ear. "There is a glow inside of that tree." Then she stepped off the branch and floated toward the trunk she was watching.

Bo followed her. In a moment's time, Twig was touching her little hands to the bark of a tree. She pressed her eyes to the wood. Then she looked at Bo. "Look inside of the tree."

He searched the fog before doing as she said. He gasped at the sight. Between the cracks in the bark, there was a moving glow. A fairy floated inside the tree. He spun toward Twig. "There is a room in there. With fairies inside-"

Twig's hand covered his mouth. She pinned him to the tree. "Shhhhh-"

Click, a door opened. Twig fell forward. Bo's hands wrapped around her waist. They fell into a dark room. They landed on a wood floor. A door locked behind them. Twig and Bo looked around in the darkness.

"Twig," Bo called out, ready to fight. He was ready to shove her behind him. Bo just needed to know where the attackers would come from.

"You are fairies." A voice spoke from the darkness, and they both spun toward it.

The voice spoke again. "Where do you come from?"

"Who are you?" Twig asked.

"We asked you first," the voice said.

Twig stepped forward into the darkness. "You first, because I like my question better. Who are you?" she asked.

Bo swallowed at her tone. If there was more than one attacker, he was not sure Twig should make them angry. Bo could only protect her from so many hands.

A long silence followed before another voice spoke from the darkness. "Twig?"

Bo felt her hands lower as she spoke. "Devin?"

The fairy standing before them dropped a leaf on the floor, uncovering his wings.

One after another, the room filled with fairy wings. Then, someone uncovered a table filled with jars of glowing fairy dust. The whole room filled with light.

Twig looked around. Fairies of all shapes and sizes filled the room. The walls were wood, making it clear they were inside the tree now.

The fairy from before spoke Twig's name again.

Bo was tense as he watched her step forward and speak. "Devin. I'm glad we found you." She smiled, and Bo frowned. She went on, "Is it safe to say this is the front line of the battle?"

Bo truly looked around now. His father's generals were standing between his guards, filling the whole tree. He now felt foolish for not seeing them sooner.

"Yes," Devin answered. "But what are you doing here?"

Twig held up the bag. "We have your...plant."

Bo saw his father's most trusted general step forward. Every fairy gasped or cheered. They all knew what the plant could do.

Devin looked past his sister, "Who is we?"

Bo pulled his shoulders back. All eyes looked at him. Twig watched him. She saw again how much bigger Bo was than most fairies. Their future king stepped forward and shook Devin's hand. She watched her brother gasp at the tight hold.

Devin bowed. "My future king, forgive me for not seeing you sooner." Everyone but Twig bowed.

Bo shrugged and took the praise gracefully. Up close, he could now see that the soldier was Twig's brother. Suddenly, he did not care how well Twig knew Devin. He turned to Twig's brother. "Think nothing of it. Now, where are my father's generals?"

Four fairies with gray hair stepped forward. At first, they tried to force Twig out of the tight circle. But Bo spoke over them and let her stay close to his side.

Twig watched as Bo and the generals talked about everything that had happened. There was a table of maps and paper in front of them. Twig stood as close to the table as she could. She loved her job serving the king, but in these last few days, she also enjoyed the thrill of this mission.

She listened to the generals speak. They were not surprised that a group of dark fairies had attacked Bo and Twig on the trail.

They knew that a troll had left with the dark fairies. The group had been planning to steal the plant from the castle. They would have needed more trolls if they planned to attack the whole kingdom. The generals agreed that the dark fairies must have decided to hurry ahead of the troll.

"It's a good thing that they split off." Devin pointed out. "I don't think two fairies could have handled a troll and the dark fairies."

Bo's eyes shot toward Twig. He wondered for a moment if his gifts would come to light now.

Of course, Twig said nothing. Twig nodded to her brother. "Yes, it is a good thing." The two siblings had never been close, and Twig did not think anyone in this room knew they were family.

Bo went on. "For now, we need to talk about the trolls and how to use this plant against them."

"Of course." One of the generals said. He started by showing how the army had already slowed down the trolls. The soldiers had been waiting on this plant and hoped that it would find its way to the front lines.

"How many trolls are there?" Bo asked.

Devin sighed, "We do not know. Every time we trap them or trick them, more just come from the fog."

Bo turned and pulled Twig towards him. "How are we going to use this against them?"

"My...sister?" Devin said slowly.

Bo's cheeks turned red. "No..." He cut the bag off her waist. "This." He set the plant on the table.

Everyone closed around the glowing petals.

The oldest general had a long white beard and big glasses. He spoke. "You need to plant it, sir. It must be in the ground, and then its roots will spread for miles. They will grow more flowers and keep the trolls far away."

Bo looked at the old fairy. "How long does it take to grow?"

The old fairy laughed. "Well, sir, it is magic. All you need to do is plant it in the dirt. The magic will take care of the rest."

Twig watched as the tired soldiers cheered. Then the old fairy's face fell. "Still...it will take more than this one plant. We will need to find the others-"

The walls of the great room broke open. Bark and wood rained down on the fairies as the trolls attacked. Madness filled the air as fairies shot out of the broken tree. Troll roars filled the dark and foggy air.

Bo shouted as he shoved pieces of wood off his shoulders. "Twig!"

Glowing fairy wings filled the air. Everywhere he looked, Bo saw trolls beating at the fairies. Little pairs of wings crashed into the trees.

Devin yelled from somewhere in the darkness. "They are charging out of the forest!"

Bo shouted again. "Twig!"

A troll used his body to break the rest of the tree in two. Bo fell out of the broken door and into the cold night air. Below him, jars of fairy dust and maps covered the wet ground of the forest. A fairy crashed into him. They both spun and landed in a pile beside the shattered tree. "Hey!" Bo shoved the fairy off of him.

Devin had been the one to land on Bo. Now Devin picked himself up and yelled above the noise of the trolls. "Bo, they are attacking us!"

"I can see that!" Bo shouted as his eyes went wide. The foggy night sky was lit with fairies.

Devin pointed past the glowing battle. "But look!"

Bo gasped. Another group of trolls had come out of the fog. "They are keeping us busy while the rest get away."

Devin shouted, "They are going to attack the kingdom!" He ducked as a branch nearly crushed him. "What do we do, sir?"

Bo shook his head. The trolls were getting ahead of the fairy army. If they got away, there would be no stopping them, and the kingdom would be lost.

Bo spun and grabbed Devin's shoulders. "Where is the plant?!"

"I don't know. The last thing I saw was Twig hugging it to her chest." Devin pulled a knife from his belt. "But for all I know, a troll has already eaten her."

"Don't say that!" Bo bit out and searched the sky for the little fairy. "Twig!"

Devin grabbed Bo's arm and spun him around. "Listen to yourself. She will never hear you over all these screaming trolls! We have to find the plant. My sister has to wait!"

Bo swallowed and nodded. Devin's eyes looked red as he added, "I'll go search the floor of the forest." Then he spun and charged into the dark sky. Bo saw Devin stab a troll, and then his wings faded into the dark. He was gone, lost in the fog.

Everything in Bo was torn. He was scared. He wanted to find Twig. He wished Devin was still with him, but Bo knew what he had to do. He needed to find the plant.

The group of trolls that were running out of the forest were nearly past the fog. There was not much time left to save themselves or the kingdom.

Bo took a deep breath and pressed his hands together. He let his anger fill him. Bo was using his magic on himself. He let out a scream of rage and hissed as he flew toward the broken tree stump. It was the last place he and Devin had seen Twig.

One troll stood guarding the empty army post. He beat at any fairy that got close. Bo slipped across the ground and pressed his hands to the troll's bare feet. The troll screamed in fear, and his cries echoed across the foggy battlefield.

Two more fairies circled his head. They blinded him with the glow of their wings until he passed out and crashed into the ground. Only then did his cries stop. The fairies moved on, fighting troll after troll.

Bo focused on his anger and climbed the tree stump. He rolled into the empty room where they had just been standing. He shoved the table out of the way and kicked jars of dust across the broken floor. "Twig!" he cried out.

He spun around the room. Nothing, nothing, nothing...he stopped.

There! Under a map! Bo shot across the room and grabbed the bag. "Twig! I found it!" He cried out in joy. Then it hit him again; he had no idea where she was. He called out again. "Twig!" But he could see that she was not under the broken walls of the room.

She was out there in the battle, or worse. Bo swallowed and ran towards the broken door. He needed to get the plant into the dirt. After that, he could let himself find Twig.

Bo jumped down from the tree trunk and flew over the troll's body. Suddenly, something smashed his face into the mud. He spun on his knees. Bo's hands were raised, ready to use his magic.

It was Twig. Her bruised face was glowing from the plant at his feet. "Twig!" he cried in relief. His face split into a smile. Then, he remembered his job. "Here. Help me dig. We need to plant this and-"

"No!" Twig grabbed his hand and held the plant tightly as she started to fly. She was pulling Bo up with her. "We can not plant this here!"

Bo flew with her as they began to pass trolls and other fairies. "What? What are you saying? We need to stop this before the trolls make it out of the fog!"

They split around a troll's head, and Bo was nearly struck down. Twig grabbed his arm and pointed ahead of them. "Look, Bo! They already have!"

Twig was right. A group of trolls had already made it out of the fog. They were charging down the path. The trolls were running straight for the kingdom.

Twig pulled on Bo and kept shouting as she flew. "I found the old general who was talking. He said we need to bury the plant ahead of the trolls. Otherwise, it will only stop the ones behind it, not the trolls on the path."

"The other trolls would still be headed for the kingdom?" Bo asked.

Twig nodded as they swooped around a troll. "If they make it off the path and split off into the woods, we will never be able to hunt them down. The trolls will reach the kingdom before we can stop them!" Twig swiped at a cut in her head. Blood was still running across her lip.

"We need to plant it ahead of them!" Bo shouted. He pressed with all his strength to speed up. Twig nodded, and the two fairies shot down the path. They flew as fast as they could. But Twig and Bo could see they were not fast enough to catch up with the trolls.

"We can't get any closer!" Bo shouted.

Twig cried out in fear. "If the path gets wider and they spread out, we will never be able to stop them!"

Bo shook his head. "No!" He wiped the sweat from his eyes and searched madly for an answer.

"Bo..." Twig gasped for breath. "I-I don't know what to do."

He thought back to their fight with the troll and the last time they had saved each other. Now they needed to save their home, but how...He yelled at Twig. "I am going to throw you, like last time!"

"What?" she cried.

Bo wanted to give Twig a second, but he could not wait. A troll at the front of the group tripped on a fallen branch. The pack of trolls slowed down. This was their chance.

Bo grabbed Twig's legs and spun around. With all his strength, Bo threw Twig down the path. She flew over the trolls' heads.

Twig choked on dirt as everything seemed to slow down. The trolls were below her. She could hear Bo's voice. But it was faded and blurry. Twig shook her head clear and shot forward.

With the speed Bo gave her, she dipped down and put more and more room between her and the trolls. Sweat poured into her eyes as she pulled out her knife. "Just a little faster...," she hissed.

A troll from behind screamed in fear. Twig looked back and saw the troll stumble. He slowed the group for a second or two. She knew that the troll's scream came from Bo using his gifts.

"Now," with a flap of her wings, Twig shot forward one more time and then landed. She rolled and dug her knife into the dirt. Twig began to cut away at the wet ground. She shook as the troll's booming feet grew closer. Twig dragged the plant from the bag and shoved it into the hole.

"Arrrrgggggg!" the biggest troll lifted his foot. He planned to smash her as she pulled the last of the dirt over the plant's roots.

"Twig!" Bo's scream echoed in Twig's ears as the foot came down on her and the plant.

Then, everything went dark.

CHAPTER 9

Bo watched as the red curls in Twig's bun blew in the wind. He and Twig rode with Devin and the general on the back of a dove.

Twig's eyes were still shut, and he wondered when she would wake up.

Below him and all around him, soldiers flew. The fairies who were hurt or dead rode on the back of doves. The rest of the army flew beside the birds.

In a few days, they would get back to the kingdom. They would bring the news of victory to the King.

When Twig buried the plant, its roots and vines had shot up from the ground. The plant built a wall so high it touched the shoulders of the trolls. But the thing that kept the trolls back was the flowers. The glow and smell showed the plant's magic. The trolls could not stand it.

For miles, the wall covered the woods around the foggy lands. The wall did end, but it would take the trolls a very long time to find their freedom.

Bo's home was safe for now.

He laid back against the feathers of the bird. He wished for sleep. The sun would rise in a few hours, and then they would see how badly Twig was hurt.

Her wing was torn. When the wall had burst up, it had thrown the trolls backward. The wall had cut Twig's wing. Not all the way, but she would be stuck on the ground for a while.

All Bo needed was for Twig to wake up. Then he could see that she was okay, and maybe he could finally get some rest himself.

"I'm afraid, sir, that this is not the end," the general spoke. Bo turned to him. He had been the one who had told Twig they needed to put the plant ahead of the trolls.

"What?" Bo asked. The general was old but very wise. Bo trusted him. The old fairy swallowed. "Sir...there were no dark fairies in the woods."

Bo thought back to the fight. "You are right...and we know the trolls were working with them. So where do you think they are?" His voice was low as they flew through the darkness.

Twig moaned in her sleep. Bo did not use his gift of happiness on her. He wanted to, but he had promised to never use his gift without her knowing.

"There are other plants, sir," the general said.

Bo turned his eyes from Twig and looked back at the old fairy. "What? Does my father know? And how do you know?"

The general went on. "Your father hoped...we both hoped this plant would make a wall as far as we need. But it didn't. We know the trolls are working with the dark fairies. I am sure that my research of old magic is right. There are other magical plants. I believe the dark fairies are hunting them down right now."

Bo was silent as the truth hit him.

The wall *did* end. The trolls could get around it. It was only a matter of time before they came back. Bo would be lying to himself if he truly believed the kingdom was safe. He swallowed. "Why are the dark fairies looking for the other plants?"

"The wall will always have a hole in it until all the plants are joined together," the general said. "The dark fairies know that. This is why they were hunting down the one you and Twig had."

Bo had left half of the army at the wall to guard it. The general was clear that once the plant was in the ground, only great magic could uproot it. Still, Bo did not want to take any chances. He was right to trust himself. He watched Twig as he spoke. "How many plants are there?"

"I've heard of four. We have already used one."

Bo fell silent. The dark fairies were still out there. The trolls still had a way to get to his kingdom. They had done a great thing today...but it was clear that this war was not over.

Twig moaned again, and Bo's voice sounded harsh. "Do you know how to find the others?"

"I have some ideas, yes. When we get back to the kingdom, we can meet with your father. For now, sir, you should rest and enjoy your victory on the battlefield. We are all proud of you. And Twig."

Bo only nodded. Another time, the praise would have meant more. But now he was just tired.

"I'll leave you to rest." The wise general slipped off the wing of the dove and joined the rest of the army. Devin had been sitting by the old fairy and listening. Now, he nodded, too, and followed the general.

That left Bo and Twig alone. Bo wished she would just wake up. Bo wanted to go home and not worry about more plants or danger-

Twig's voice stopped his thinking, and he jumped as she spoke. "What happened?"

"Don't sit up too fast." He pressed her back down on the dove feathers when she tried to rise.

"Why? What happened, Bo?" She looked around. The glow of her broken wing shone in her green eyes. She could see the army flying around them. "Did we win?" she asked.

Bo took a deep breath and told her everything. He showed her the broken wing and talked about the other plants they would need to find.

Twig listened and nodded. She was staring at the leaves wrapped around her wing when she spoke. "So... it's not over?"

Bo shook his head. "I'm sorry, but no."

Twig swallowed. "But we won today?"

Bo stared at the broken wing. "Because of you."

"And you," she pointed out. Then she moaned from the pain in her wing.

"Do you want me to..." Bo held out his hands.

It took Twig a moment to understand that he was offering to use his gifts on her. She shivered at the memory of the dark fairy's attack. "Thanks, but...I need more time before I feel a fairy's gift again. Even if it is happiness."

Bo nodded and looked down at his tan hands. "I understand. I would feel the same way."

"Hey." Twig poked his big shoulder. "It's not about you. If it were, I wouldn't insist on helping you find the others." After hearing about the other plants, Twig knew she wanted to help find them.

Bo lifted his eyebrows. The idea of having Twig help him was more than he had hoped for. "You really want to help?"

Twig laughed. She had no idea how much her offer touched Bo. Then she groaned as more pain ran up her back. "I am the royal messenger. And...I would have trouble with the idea of not being a part of the next mission." A blush ran up her cheeks. She was not normally so honest about her need for control.

Now, it was Bo's turn to laugh. "Right, right. I did promise that I would make sure to invite you next time."

Twig smiled. "So it's a deal?"

"You are the king's messenger, after all."

The end.

Made in United States
North Haven, CT
09 December 2024

62051259R00059